To Aaro, Eino, Rania
and to all the tomtes – H.T.

To Olli, Joel, Saul, Silja, Elisa,
Riikka-Maria, Juhani, Anna-Liisa and to Kyösti – I.K.

Little Tomte's
CHRISTMAS
WISH

Inkeri Karvonen
and Hannu Taina

Little Tomte lived in a cosy house.
Just outside his cosy house
was a group of trees, which grew
together like one big tree.

When Little Tomte walked
under his tree, he felt like
he was in a forest.

The tree was always changing,
and full of surprises.

In spring, bright new leaves grew, and a wonderful fragrance filled the air.

In summer, the leaves and branches made a green sunshade. Little Tomte loved to sit under them in his favourite chair. The birds sang from dawn till dusk, and sometimes even in the night. Or was it the tree singing in the breezes and the sunshine and the warm dark?

In autumn, the leaves turned red, brown and gold, like fire. Little Tomte collected the most beautiful ones and spread them on his table. They kept glowing, long after the tree's branches were bare and black.

One wintery day it started to snow. White flakes piled softly on the tree's branches outside.

Little Tomte started waiting for Christmas.

Little Tomte cleared snow from outside his door. He wondered about making a snow tomte beside his gate. He sat by the window and hoped for Christmas.

Night came. He stepped out and stared at the stars.
He felt small and lonely, and he made a Christmas wish:
"Even though it's only me, please let Christmas come."

The next day, Little Tomte
thought, "I'll sing some songs.
That will feel like Christmas."

So he sang a Christmas carol,
but his voice sounded quiet
and lost on its own.

The next day, Little Tomte had a new plan. "I know, I'll bake some ginger Christmas cookies! That will feel like Christmas." But when he opened the syrup jar, it was empty.

"I'll make some Christmas pastries instead," he thought, "with plum jam filling." But he found he'd eaten all the jam.

"I'll cook some Christmas porridge then," he decided. But he remembered he'd lent his big pot to the field mice for their harvest festival.

Little Tomte felt sorry for himself. "Christmas will never come now," he thought. "I don't even have any presents." He huddled on his stool and evening fell.

It got so dark that Little Tomte lit a candle.
The golden light spread around his house, and
fell on the snow outside his window. His tree
glowed. Suddenly he knew what to do.

He would make Christmas candles!
All night long he dipped wicks
into melted wax, and by morning
smooth, warm-smelling candles
filled his big basket.

Little Tomte opened the door to see the dawn and – what a surprise! – there in
the snow was a big porridge pot, with some syrup and a jar of plum jam inside it!
He could make his ginger Christmas cookies, plum pastries and porridge after all.

A clear, still evening arrived and Little Tomte carried his Christmas candles and treats out to his tree. He fixed shining candles to every branch, so they glimmered and sparkled, lighting up the night sky.

Soon he heard muffled footsteps and whispering voices. Everyone had seen the beautiful tree! They came from miles around, over the hills and dales, and they all brought presents.

Little Tomte and his friends and neighbours sang
Christmas carols joyfully together. They shared the
cookies, pastries and porridge, which tasted delicious
in the cold air.

   Then each visitor carried one of Little Tomte's
glowing candles home, making trails of golden light
from his tree, over the river and across the hills, as
far as he could see.

Back inside his cosy house, Little Tomte opened his presents, and smiled.

He had wished for Christmas, and Christmas had come!
It had arrived under his tree, like a light in the darkness.

First published in Finnish as *Pienen Tontun Ihmeellinen Joulu* by Werner Söderström Osakeyhtiö, Helsinki, in 2004
First published in English by Floris Books in 2013

Text © 2004 by Inkeri Karvonen
Illustrations © 2004 by Hannu Taina
English edition © 2013 Floris Books
British Library CIP Data available
ISBN 978-178250-016-2
Printed in Malaysia